THE UMBRELLA THAT CHANGED THE WORLD

BY BERN CLAY

ILLUSTRATIONS BY DIANE MICKLIN

BALBOA.PRESS

A DIVISION OF HAY HOUSE

Balboa Press books may be ordered through booksellers or by contacting:

Balboa Press
A Division of Hay House
1663 Liberty Drive
Bloomington, IN 47403
www.balboapress.com
844-682-1282

Because of the dynamic nature of the Internet, any web addresses or links contained in this book may have changed since publication and may no longer be valid. The views expressed in this work are solely those of the author and do not necessarily reflect the views of the publisher, and the publisher hereby disclaims any responsibility for them.

The author of this book does not dispense medical advice or prescribe the use of any technique as a form of treatment for physical, emotional, or medical problems without the advice of a physician, either directly or indirectly. The intent of the author is only to offer information of a general nature to help you in your quest for emotional and spiritual well-being. In the event you use any of the information in this book for yourself, which is your constitutional right, the author and the publisher assume no responsibility for your actions.

Any people depicted in stock imagery provided by Getty Images are models, and such images are being used for illustrative purposes only. Certain stock imagery © Getty Images.

Print information available on the last page.

ISBN: 978-1-9822-6683-7 (sc)
ISBN: 978-1-9822-6685-1 (hc)
ISBN: 978-1-9822-6684-4 (e)

Library of Congress Control Number: 2021907214

Balboa Press rev. date: 05/03/2021

For the men in my life…Ganky,

Creaky, Mushy and Button.

You are the blessed change in my world...

This one is special, he thought.. *Look how he shines!*

In a hot, airless factory, in a manufacturing city outside of China, Old Man had perfected his craft. His gnarled fingers reached into a bin on a conveyer belt and he easily caught the blue-black swatch of silk fabric. He expertly stretched the shiny black membrane over the metal frame until it was transformed into a perfect umbrella.

Where will you go, my finest creation? Old Man pondered.

Looking far down the line, filled with other somber workers, he saw a huge shipping container with the words, USA and NEW YORK CITY in bold letters. Old Man's heart leapt knowing that this magnificent work of art would find a home in a free world.

Old Man's age and the circumstances of his birth had erased any hope or ambition. When he was young, Old Man had dreams of a life that was devoted to helping others. He longed to become a doctor but his fate had been decided by a faceless and crushing bureaucracy. Old Man has worked in the umbrella factory since he was nine years old. It has been a brutal and ruthless existence and yet he endured. Day by day, month by month, year by year and now decade by decade, he labored. Although he had lived his entire life under the heartlessness of an authoritarian government, Old Man was grateful that he had been assigned any position. He had been able to provide a meager existence for himself and his precious wife.

Knowing this was his final day of work, Old Man felt a tug of fear. Not because of the gnawing hunger ever-present in his stomach but for his fragile and ailing wife. He allowed himself the luxury of a fleeting pause in his work and considered their bleak future and a sigh escaped.

Old Man's lull in the relentless task caught the ever-watchful eye of the dreaded Team Leader. Pounding footsteps approached, as Old Man's trembling hands gently lowered Umbrella onto the conveyor belt.

Before Team Leader reached him, Old Man whispered these words, like a prayer, "Be the change you wish to see in the World, Umbrella!"

Old Man watched his last creation slowly disappear into a sea of colors and aluminum. Old Man's bequest to Umbrella was the final act of his open heart. As Old Man braced for the certain punishment of Team Leader, he bowed his head in submission. Out of the corner of his eye, Old Man saw the glimmering Umbrella riding tall upon the heap of other umbrellas, and experienced a rare feeling ... Hope.

A world away, life was fabulous for Umbrella. He lived in a display window of a posh department store on 5th Avenue in New York City. Umbrella rested casually against the leg of a tuxedoed man. The faux man's name was Mannequin. The duo was featured in an elaborate and spectacular garden wedding scene. The tuxedoed gentleman leaned against a flowered trellis and had his arms crossed in a sort of bored authority. Mannequin sported a tailored tuxedo and very expensive sunglasses. There was a beam of light, representing the sun, which shone directly on Umbrella and Mannequin. The black fabric of both of their outfits seemed to shimmer under the warm glow of the artificial afternoon. Mannequin's cool gaze was directed to the far corner of the display window. There, a sprinkler system had been cleverly retrofitted to deliver a sudden downpour.

Inside the amazing display window, a beautiful bride and her handsome groom were forever escaping from a wet disaster. The bride's lace-encased arm was lifted over her head in a feeble attempt to keep her fake hair dry while her groom followed to shield his newly-minted love. His outstretched arm had been positioned to appear protective and the groom's other arm was being utilized to drag a very uncooperative and adorable ring-bearer to dry shelter.

Mannequin and Umbrella seemed to look with disdain at the foolishness before them. Their calm amidst the soggy mayhem made them appear snobby and aloof. Sadly, Umbrella and Mannequin were not acting, especially Umbrella.

Look at those fools, thought Umbrella. *If only she married my guy,* mused Umbrella heartlessly. *Mannequin is the perfect man. Plus he has fabulous me!*

Swarms of tourists and just as many native New Yorkers stopped and gazed at the scene. Everyone seemed taken in by the drama played out before them. Phones and cameras were pulled out and pictures were snapped and posted to the digital world. Even the most jaded of city dwellers seem touched by the bittersweet tableau.

Mannequin and Umbrella quite liked the attention. They were a smug dynamic duo. Naturally, Umbrella was convinced that the crowds came only to see them. They appeared to share a similar contempt and cynical delight for the plight of the soaked wedding party in the far corner. Day after day of watching the bride, groom and pugnacious ring bearer endure twelve hours of drenching precipitation had not softened Umbrella's or Mannequin's hearts.

Perhaps an inside wedding would have been the smarter plan, thought Umbrella with a sarcastic grin.

The display window conveyed the very best and very worse of a day that was planned as a joyous celebration. The purposeful disengagement of the dry Mannequin with the much-needed Umbrella contrasted the fleeing and rain-soaked trio captured even the most distracted and cynical commuter. Angry faces were instantly transformed as they walked by the wedding window.

All of this was lost on Umbrella. He certainly coveted all of the attention that had come his way but he despised the people on the outside. Umbrella had grown bored of people staring, pointing and taking his picture. He especially hated it when the little ones pressed their faces against the window. When their mothers pulled them away, it always left a smudge. Sometimes their little handprints made it impossible for Umbrella to stare at himself in the reflection of the glass and this annoyed him.

Umbrella never grew tired of gazing at himself. The lights in the window illuminated his fabric, making it shimmer. Although there wasn't anything to do, except lean against

Mannequin, Umbrella shuddered at the thought of being out there with those awful people. He had seen how the masses treated others like him. *Imagine me in the dirty hands of a nobody,* he thought. Inside the dry and safe display window, Umbrella lived a protected and privileged existence.

I was designed for better things. Hmph! That Old Man who created me told me so, Umbrella sulked.

As the weeks passed, Umbrella would think about his creator. He would become very frustrated.

That silly Old Man, he fretted. *Why would I want to change anything in my world? I know Mannequin doesn't talk or anything, but at least he isn't bending me or opening me up and twisting my spines! Be the change you want to see in the world. No thank you!*

The lights in the window began to dim and another wet and ruined wedding day commenced.

About once a day, usually before the sun was up and crowds would pause to take pictures, a young man would come through the display. His name was Dante. Umbrella knew this because a screaming lady dressed in black would yell his name every time she came into the display window. Each morning, Dante would dust and sweep and make subtle alterations to the Wedding Scene. He placed fresh flowers on the table, adjusted the bride's train, fiddled with the ring bearer's mini bowtie, and regulated the flow of the rain so it didn't create a flood.

Dante had a dreamy and gentle way about him. He walked gingerly through the scene, careful not to disturb anything. He rarely made changes to Mannequin and Umbrella. He always seemed to be working in the far corner.

I guess we are just perfect, thought Umbrella.

One morning though, Dante picked up Umbrella and placed him on the table behind Mannequin. Dante stared at the change he made to the scene for a very long time. He held his fingers under a hairless chin, and considered the adjustment, as a great artist might, when looking at a painting. Changing his mind, Dante shook his head a little, and carefully returned Umbrella to his leaning position against Mannequin's leg.

This morning began in a similar way but suddenly, a scream broke Dante's reverie. The tiny woman, dressed entirely in black, was back! She charged toward the timid, young man. She screamed at him, calling him rudderless and lazy. Her arms flailed as she shrieked that Dante would never be anything but a feckless art student. With that, she picked up Umbrella and flung it at Dante. Umbrella smacked Dante right across his face.

Not checking to see if she hurt Dante, she icily said, "You are so fired. Get out!" Turning on her stilettos she stomped out of the display window.

A crowd of people had gathered and witnessed the entire temper tantrum of the terrifying woman. Cameras had been pulled out and videos were about to be posted which would guarantee worldwide humiliation for the unfortunate art student. Dante turned crimson in embarrassment. Spying what his vile boss had flung at him, he scooped Umbrella up from the floor and opened him up. Now camouflaged by Umbrella, he backed away from the mocking eyes and taunts of the crowd. Protected by Umbrella, he slipped out of the display window. Dante ran to the back of the store, out the employee's entrance and into a narrow alley. Walking slowly and sadly in the direction of home, Dante realized he had forgotten to grab his jacket. But even worse, he had forgotten something else. In Dante's clenched fist was none other than the Umbrella that was made to change the world!

Oh no, he thought. *I can't go back! Dragon Lady has probably told Security.*

Dante looked down at Umbrella and lifted up the price tag. 110.00 dollars!

What do I do now? I will be arrested if I go back. Dante was truly frightened. Dante walked slowly through the streets toward the edge of his campus. He had never taken anything in his life.

Dante had worked so hard at the posh department store. He loved transforming a blank space into something alive and full of excitement. He knew the purpose of the window display was to subtly advertise the store's merchandise but he had loved the opportunity to show off his creativity. Dante had hoped all of the early mornings and super late nights might turn into a permanent position for him after graduation. Other than his vile boss, everyone liked Dante and saw his talent and promise.

I guess I will have to go to the Dean's office and tell them that I was fired. I don't even know what I did. What will my parents think?

Dante shuffled down the crowded city block, almost in a daze. So many thoughts were buzzing through his brain.

He clutched Umbrella, holding onto him for strength. *What am I going to do?* he wondered.

However, Umbrella was elated. He ignored Dante's sorrow. Umbrella felt a jolt of excitement being on the outside! He had never been anywhere but the shipping container and then the window display. Dante sat down on a hard bench and continued to hold Umbrella against his chest. Umbrella could hear music from the cars whizzing by and the rapid beating of the art student's heart. Umbrella didn't care about poor Dante or his sad circumstances. All Umbrella cared about was himself.

What a world!, Umbrella thought in amazement.

It was so loud and filled with sounds, smells, colors, and people. *There are so many people,* Umbrella mused. Umbrella was out in the city, among the very same people he and Mannequin would sneer at and find so beneath them. The glass that had kept Umbrella sealed within the fake wedding day that Dante had created, also kept Umbrella safe from everything in real life. Suddenly the smug little Umbrella felt quite unsure about himself and his future. Umbrella felt a growing resentment toward Dante.

Why did this fired art student take me out of the window? What is going to happen to me, Umbrella whined to himself.

He pushed one of his spines into Dante's chest.

"Ouch!" said Dante.

As Dante looked up from his dark thoughts he caught the eye of a pretty girl walking by the bench.

"Hey," she said softly. "Hi ..." stuttered Dante.

Without being invited, she sat down on the bench and looked at the downtrodden student.

"Dante, it's me, Daisy from Watercolor Class. Why haven't you called me?" she asked softly.

Dante and Umbrella looked at sweet Daisy. She was dressed in a green tie-dye dress with combat boots and had a burlap sack flung across one shoulder. Her blonde hair was windswept and shiny and her perfume smelled like lavender. She had several shiny bracelets on her wrist that made a soft chime sound when she moved.

"I had a great time at the Met that night!" she said. Dante stammered,

"I'm sorry, but I have been busy with that Internship, you know the one on 5th Avenue." Dante's voice wavered.

Hey, thought Umbrella, *she likes you*! *But you are wasting my time! I have to get going and change the world!*

"That's ok," said Daisy. "How is it going? My roommate told me about the wedding scene. She said it was genius!"

Dante exhaled a deep sigh. "Yeah, thanks but I got fired and I ran out with this expensive parting gift!" he confessed.

He held Umbrella near his chest like a shield.

"What happened, Dante?" asked Daisy.

Looking into Daisy's kind eyes made Dante feel brave. He told Daisy the whole embarrassing story. Daisy was even able to make Dante laugh about his mean boss. When Dante was finished, Daisy leaned in and took a look at Umbrella.

Picking up Umbrella's price tag she let out a low whistle, "Wow, what a fancy thing!" she laughed.

You have no idea. What would she know about anything upscale with her thrift store outfit, thought Umbrella cruelly.

"Listen, Dante. My Mom told me a really cool fable when I was little. She said that there were a limited number of umbrellas in the world just like bikes in the city and that neither really belonged to anyone. Umbrellas and bikes get passed around so the people who need them can use them. Bikes and umbrellas are things that have been created to make life simpler. To help us, right?"

"You don't need to feel bad about taking the umbrella. It was a happy accident. Just leave it here and the next time it rains, someone will come along, needing an umbrella and you will be someone's hero!" she said joyfully.

"Isn't that called rationalization? After all, it was over 100 bucks!" asked Dante.

"Leave it," she commanded. "You will make someone happy. Besides, it's good karma."

She stood up and held out her hand. Dante placed Umbrella onto the bench, reached for Daisy's soft hand and stood up. They walked towards campus leaving Umbrella, alone, lying on the bench.

Wait, what about me? How am I going to show my greatness to the world on this dirty bench, sulked Umbrella.

He just lay there pouting and feeling sorry for himself.

The sun was shining so no one noticed the stray Umbrella. Occasionally a bus would drive by, or a jogger but Umbrella really had no idea where he was and how he was getting off the dirty bench. After a few hours, Umbrella heard laughter and music behind him. Umbrella tried to spin himself around.

Frustrated, Umbrella thought, *How am I going to change the world if I am incapable of changing direction?*

Cars were speeding by and his fabric flapped. Several large SUVS zoomed by and Umbrella was lifted off the bench.

That dumb art student left me open, he thought nervously.

A city bus drove past and Umbrella's spines opened up. His fabric started to flap and he flipped over and somersaulted off the bench. Now Umbrella was almost completely open. He heard a distant wailing. It grew louder and louder. A huge red fire truck sped by and in its wake, Umbrella was lifted into the air.

This is it! This is my destiny! I am going to change the world through flight! I will be famous! The first umbrella that can fly!

A gust of wind caught him and Umbrella was flipping into the air, high above the Campus.

I am amazing! Whee!

He looked down. No one even noticed him. Umbrella soared over the football field. He looked down at the players and their fans.

Hey, look at me! I am the Umbrella who changed the world! Why aren't they cheering for me, he wondered.

Picking up speed, Umbrella tumbled through in the air over the engineering building.

Hey, geeks, he thought unkindly. *Check out my Applied AeroDynamic Principles! Why aren't they applauding?*

With that, Umbrella smacked handle-first into the smokestack that was attached to the garbage building.

Ugh, it smells like cabbage and old socks, thought a disgusted Umbrella.

Before he could say another snarky word, Umbrella felt himself falling, fast, and suddenly everything went black.

"Frank, you kill me!" cackled an unfamiliar voice.

Umbrella gained consciousness in the calloused grip of someone. She smelled like day-old chicken. Umbrella was moving in some kind of a tube and there were a lot of people around him. Some standing, some sitting, others hanging onto poles.

Ugh more people, thought Umbrella.

Umbrella looked around and realized he was on a bus.

Dreadful mode of transportation, he thought. *Mannequin had a limousine!*

He saw that the people were all staring at something ahead of them. No one was talking. Some of them were asleep. Occasionally, a disembodied voice would call out a street name but Umbrella was still in Mary's grip so he was stuck.

Really, thought Umbrella, *hanging with these people will not make me famous.*

He felt sore and remembered hitting the smokestack.

I hope I am not too hurt to fly again. Fame awaits, Umbrella pondered confidently.

With his thoughts dedicated to his celebrity, Umbrella dozed off. He woke to the firm grip and abrasive sound of Mary's voice. Reluctantly, he listened to her story for a moment.

☂

"Where I really want to go and bring my bunch with me is to see the Statue of Liberty." she said wistfully.

"Why there, Mary? There are plenty of sights to show them in the city!" asked BusDriver Frank.

Umbrella could feel a deep sigh escape Mary. "You know why, Frank. Their father was a firefighter on the worst day. I don't want to take them anywhere near that place. Maybe one day, but not yet. I want to show them a symbol of hope and possibility."

Then she bent down and reached into the messy bag she was carrying and pulled out a pamphlet. Umbrella looked at the wrinkled brochure and saw before him something so magnificent and awesome that he gasped. He could hear Mary with her endless chatter when all he wanted to do was find out who this magnificent and noble lady was and how to find her!

Look at how tall she stands! The entire world can probably see her! She is holding a flamed torch for all to see! It all makes sense now! I was created to cover her in case of rain! I will be the most famous umbrella on the planet! Umbrella was convinced that this was the change in the world Old Man had prophesied.

"So after ten hours on my feet, dishing out carrots and steak to a bunch of spoiled college kids, smack, this little guy falls out of the sky and hits me on my head," she cackled and started to cough.

Umbrella saw that the bus was almost empty and that Mary with the vise-like grip was still talking to BusDriver Frank.

"Mary, you should play the lottery, tonight! It's your lucky day!" BusDriver Frank's voice rumbled in a good-natured way. "Hey maybe if you win, you can take all the kids and that lucky Umbrella and he can protect Lady Liberty from all the bad weather they get out in the harbor!"

Mary laughed just a little and wistfully said, "When their father was alive he loved to take them on adventures. My husband was the fun parent and had so many dreams for them. His love for this country led him to sacrifice his life in the protection of their freedoms. Meanwhile Umbrella was practically jumping up and down.

This is it, he thought. *Bus Driver Frank is smarter than I first thought. I am going to be the Umbrella that saves the Statue of Liberty! Since I will be above her head, everyone will know that I am more important than her! This is my destiny! I am going to be the most famous umbrella in the world!*

Mary and BusDriver Frank were still joking and talking.

"Aw Frank, thanks for cheering me up! I win the lottery every day when I go home and the kids haven't burned down the house! Here's my stop, Frank, see you tomorrow!" she practically shouted.

Mary heaved a heavy sigh and with Umbrella securely pinned under her arm, she lowered herself down the steps and onto the sidewalk.

"At least it isn't raining! You have a good night, Mary!" BusDriver Frank cheerfully shouted.

As the jovial man closed the door, Umbrella watched as the enormous bus pulled away.

Can't wait to meet her kids, Umbrella thought sarcastically. *Now how am I going to get to that statue and become the most famous Umbrella in the world?*

Mary walked slowly down the sidewalk, avoiding bikes, trash cans, and the occasional barking dog. The houses were lined up in rows that didn't allow for much sunlight or breezes. But she eagerly walked down the familiar street. Often she would wave and sometimes she would shout a friendly hello.

If I wanted to change this world, I would get some bleach, smirked Umbrella.

There is no wind. How am I going to take flight? How am I going to escape from this dreadful creature, thought the snobby Umbrella.

He was a little panicked with the notion of entering one of the small houses. Mary clutched Umbrella tightly and as she walked toward her home. She hummed a little song. She arrived at a place, not very different from the dozens of houses they had walked past. She hoisted herself onto the dingy porch and from within, there was an unimaginable loud cacophony.

"What is all of that noise! It's louder than the kitchen at the college!" she cried.

Umbrella braced himself. *Oh joy,* thought Umbrella sarcastically. *More awful people.*

Next came a tumbling, running, screaming, crying, and laughing crowd of hooligans. Five children spilled themselves upon Mary and Umbrella. Stories of the last eaten cookie, hair being pulled, milk spilled on homework, dog running away again, and the mean neighbor yelling at them pushed out of their months in a clamor that could only be described as a wail. Mary patted them, hugged them, gave directions to one and asked questions of another. This sole parent gave comfort, love, advice, discipline and security to the chaos before her. Mayhem meeting mayhem until, like a sudden summer storm, the children retreated to what they were doing before Mary got home.

"Whew!" Mary sighed smiling. "My young ones are quite a crew!".

She took off her coat and plopped down onto the worn sofa. Laying Umbrella beside her, she called out a name. A little boy appeared and she gave him a quick hug. He was Mary's youngest and everyone called him Little Brother.

"Look what Mama found today! It looks expensive, doesn't it? Be an angel and put it in the closet for me, will you?"

"Ok!" said Little Brother.

He picked Umbrella up and shoved him, roughly into the musty closet and slammed it with a bang. Stuck in a mothballed infused dark prison, Umbrella was temporarily rendered sightless. He pushed up against something wooden and dusty.

Now what, Umbrella thought.

The din outside the closet died down and drifted away to another part of the house. It became like the sound of the distant rumbling of thunder after a storm. The wooden thing slid closer to Umbrella.

Oh, I am never going to get to be the greatest Umbrella to change the World! I am going to be murdered!

Overcome by terror and the smell of mothballs, Umbrella was unable to breath. Suddenly there was the sound of a little thud. Umbrella fainted.

"You poor baby!" said the unknown object with compassion in it's deep voice. It rustled closer to Umbrella in the dark, kicking up dust as it approached.

"Are you going to hurt me?" whispered the terrified Umbrella.

Laughing so hard, the unknown object almost fell on top of Umbrella but instead knocked itself against the door. It was dark in the closet and the only light was a sliver that slipped in under the bottom of the door. Umbrella's eyes were slowly adjusting to the darkness and he started to see a blurry outline.

"Of course not! I would never hurt a fly. You are hanging with the good guys, my new friend!" the voice said kindly.

"What are you and is there anything else in here?" Umbrella asked in a rare moment of timidity.

"Good stuff, purposeful things live in closets. Things like vacuums, coats and sweaters and hangers to hold them up. There is Little Sister's Backpack over there. She is the only organized one in the whole crazy family. On the shelf is Gift Wrap from last Christmas and Uncle Al's Hat from last Sunday and boxes of pictures and school supplies..."

Umbrella interrupted the shape and asked "Which one are you?" Umbrella's voice was trembling.

Sweeping forward in one magnificent swoop, the shape said in a very dignified voice, "I'm Broom Man."

A sliver of light crept in from the top of the closet and Umbrella saw before him, a long handled broom wearing a hat. Umbrella gave Broom Man an annoyed look and said "Ha ha, really funny. By the way, I wasn't scared!"

Normally Umbrella would never think to speak to such a lowly object but after the day he had, Umbrella decided that he needed a friend. *I guess this guy will do,* he chuckled to himself.

In the ensuing hour, Umbrella told, frankly, whined to Broom Man all of his tales of woe. He angrily recalled his interactions with every person who had held him in their hand. Umbrella described Old Man who created him at the factory. He referred to his creator as a misguided idiot and a fool.

He described his posh beginnings with Mannequin and called him and the rest of the Wedding Party stupid and boring.

He referred to Dante as smelly, talentless and lacking a spine. He described Daisy as a fake hippy who bossed Dante around.

Umbrella continued to drone on about his first experience with flight, "I was a natural! I really thought that I was meant to change the world through flight. I was hoping that I would become as famous as the Wright Brothers. After all, I am definitely the only umbrella in the world who has flown."

As Umbrella rattled on and on about how life had let him down, Broom Man remained very quiet. He shifted his weight back and forth on his bristles. Hangers hung on every word of Umbrella's tale, tinkling every once in a while, and Vacuum stood stoically and silent in the corner. Gift Wrap could be heard rustling and Little Sister's Backpack edged over so that she could compare her coarse fabric with Umbrella's expensive silk. Umbrella looked down his handle at the shy backpack and when she crept closer, his expression of disdain made her scamper back to the corner. He took no notice of her embarrassment. Umbrella let out a sigh and ended the final chapter of his saga which revealed his profound lack of empathy and complete narcissism.

He said that he felt assaulted when Mary picked him up off the campus lawn. He told Broom Man and the rest of his audience that her hands smelled like cabbage and old socks and that he, the most special umbrella ever created, had lost his social standing. He saved his meanest comment for BusDriver Frank.

"That guy was basically a nobody. He was going nowhere," Umbrella finished.

The look of satisfaction and triumph on his face was shocking to everyone in the closet. Umbrella didn't notice their reactions. All that mattered was him and his quest for fame.

"You see," Umbrella announced to the members of the closet, "I was designed for better things than this! I was made to be better than other objects and other umbrellas, even! I was created," Umbrella took a well-placed pause for extra drama, "To be the change I wished to see in the World"!

It seemed as if Umbrella was begging them to acknowledge what should be obvious to all-his superiority.

"I wasn't designed to be practical like you, Hangers or you Gift Wrap, or you old, outdated Vacuum or even you, Broom Man. I was custom-made and designed for bigger and better things than all of you! So can someone please explain to me how I am going to change the world when I am stuck here with all of you losers?"

An audible gasp was heard throughout the closet. Broom Man bristled so furiously that Uncle Al's Hat fell off his head and onto the floor. Broom Man bent forward to pick up Uncle Al's Hat but instead, whacked Umbrella right across his handle.

"Hey, that hurt!" shouted Umbrella.

In a quiet voice, Broom Man said, "Sorry, but words can hurt, too, Umbrella."

"Yeah but not ..." Umbrella started to speak.

Broom Man gave Umbrella THAT look.

"Don't interrupt, Umbrella, because I have something to say to you. You have said more than enough. I need to say it not only for myself but also on behalf of all of the contents of this closet." Broom Man continued in a firm voice, "Umbrella, you certainly have had quite an adventure so far, but do you realize how fortunate you have been?"

"Fortunate?" gasped Umbrella.

"We just had to listen to your complaints and cruelty for over an hour, now it's my turn." Broom Man said sternly.

Umbrella stared and looked a little scared.

Broom Man spoke. "Yes, Umbrella you are fortunate but you are obviously suffering from what we like to call around here it's-all-about-me-world. All of us have been designed for important purposes. We aren't very fancy but we all have worth. We all have value. We care about that lady and her family and we do our best to fulfill that design plan and perform to our finest. But is that all it is? Of course not. Hangers keep all the clothes tidy and neat. GiftWrap can transform a present into something much more special. Vacuum is always cleaning up after the children. Who knows how Vacuum can recover from Christmas with all the small parts and batteries."

Broom Man looked over at Vacuum and they exchanged a smile that silently transmitted respect.

"Look at me Umbrella. I was and still am, the very best design model. Everyone in the closet looked down at Broom Man's slanted bristles and aerodynamic handle.

He was clearly wise and timeless.

Broom Man continued, "Sure I sweep up crumbs, broken glass, and pieces of paper. Do you hear me complaining about it?"

Umbrella rolled his eyes and looked away.

Broom Man continued. "Do you hear me or any of us complaining about our purpose or what we were designed to do? Well do you?" demanded the noble Broom Man.

"No" grumbled Umbrella begrudgingly.

Broom Man said, "That's right. Not one of us complains because unlike, the amazing you, Sir Umbrella, within each of us lies a sense of pride. Pride and a willingness to perform, what to you may seem as a meaningless task. Each job completed brings comfort to that lady out there. She is all alone raising those children. You see, by doing what we do, without all of the complaining and moaning, we demonstrate pride in ourselves and compassion for serving others. Each of us, in our own way, are making a change we want to see in the world, aren't we gang?"

Everyone in the closet gave a small cheer for Broom Man.

"Umbrella," Broom Man continued, "You will never fulfill your wise creator's wish for you unless you first feel for others."

"Are you done, Old Man?" snarked Umbrella. "I AM different from all of you. I was created to be BETTER than all of you!" Umbrella yelled. "I don't understand why you don't see that I am special. I think you are just jealous."

Broom Man then rustled back to the corner of the closet and leaned against the wall. "Yeah, ok Umbrella. You keep thinking that way. Good luck with changing the world!" Broom Man said sadly.

Umbrella was furious that a broom, an old dumb broom, for that matter, would have the nerve to talk to him in such a manner. *I am the Umbrella that will change the World,* thought heartless Umbrella. *How dare they think I am anything like them!*

Before he could say another selfish word, the closet door was flung open. Umbrella was grabbed. The closet door was slammed shut and out the front door Umbrella went. Stomping footsteps, screen door swinging open, now on the porch, Umbrella was blinded by the rays of the setting sun.

"Ma, I am going to the park with the guys, ok?" shouted a teenage boy.

His strong arm grabbed Umbrella by the handle and flipped him around and around until Umbrella's head was spinning. "Take Little Brother," Mary shouted back.

"Aw Ma."

"Take him" Mary repeated, "Or you aren't going anywhere!"

Little Brother, arrived on the porch and mouthed to his older sibling, "I'll tell Ma you have her fancy Umbrella unless you take me."

Big Brother gave Little Brother a slip of a smile. They ran outside and jumped on rusty, ancient bikes and rode off into the dusk.

Umbrella was clutched in the hand of Big Brother. Then he was roughly stuffed into a backpack and was now just a shocked passenger on a bike going way too fast. Umbrella could see a little as he gazed over the edge of the backpack. As they zoomed along, Umbrella spied

Little Brother in the distance. Little Brother was furiously peddling to keep up with them.

"Wait up!" Little Brother implored.

Ignored by Big Brother, the distance between the two brothers grew.

I am being kidnapped by a monster, thought Umbrella. *Look at that little kid back there. It is getting quite dark and there are lots of cars.*

Umbrella caught himself feeling concerned for Little Brother and quickly transferred that feeling to himself.

Umbrella thought, *Who cares about the little fool. If he gets hurt it's all his fault. Anyway, what kind of mother would let her children out in this neighborhood. At least I don't have to hear another of Broom Man's sermons! What's going to happen to me? How am I going to get the fame Old Man promised me? Why is everything so hard for me?* Umbrella was feeling sorry for himself. Again!

Big Brother had arrived at a place that was strange and unfamiliar to Umbrella. It seemed like a place for small children but night had fallen and all the little ones were tucked safely in their warm beds. Umbrella could see a sliding board and little fake ponies. Large shadowy figures were sprawled across them and no one was playing or having fun.

Hmph, thought Umbrella, w*hat sort of families do these dark creatures belong?*

Little Brother caught up and parked his bike next to his brother. "Why didn't you wait up?"

Big Brother gave Little Brother a minute to catch his breath.

They started to walk slowly towards the dark silhouettes.

Little Brother whispered nervously, "I don't think Ma would want us here."

Big Brother whispered, "Wait here, I just have to give something to that guy."

Umbrella was horrified. *You mean the one that looks like an actual snake?*

Again, Umbrella felt a small feeling of concern but he pushed it quickly away.

It's Big Brother's fault if anything happens to me, thought Umbrella. *Maybe he will get in trouble when he gets back to his horrible house.*

Naturally, Umbrella didn't think about Little Brother's safety. Umbrella' s immediate concern was that he didn't want to be put back in the closet with all of those pointless things.

Curled up on two swings, a shadowy teen had wrapped himself through the metal and hard rubber. He looked like a futuristic reptile. Snake gazed slowly and deliberately at the two brothers.

"What can I do for you, ladies?" Snake asked sarcastically as he flicked a lit cigarette toward the boys. His voice was cold and menacing.

The other dark figures laughed cruelly.

Big Brother walked toward Snake and said, his voice shaking, "Hi. Um Snake, I found this and I thought you would want it back."

In Big Brother's outstretched hand was a leather rope with a pendant. Snake continued to smirk until he saw what Big Brother held in his hand. He unwound himself from the play set and moved quickly toward Big Brother. Snake yanked Big Brother by his shirt until they stood only four or five inches from one another.

"Where did a little stain like you get my stuff?" hissed Snake.

Big Brother started to explain, his voice frantic with panic. "I, um, found it." Big Brother almost whispered.

An obvious good deed gone wrong, smirked Umbrella.

In a flash, Snake swiped the necklace from Big Brother's open hand. In a split second, Snake began to wallop kind Big Brother. Snake delivered blows to Big Brother's face, his back and his torso. The pain was searing. Stunned, Big Brother staggered away from Snake, and stumbled toward shocked Little Brother, Umbrella and his bike.

Looking for an escape but hoping to protect Little Brother, he mouthed "RUN".

When loyal Little Brother saw Snake and three of his shady minions closing in on Big Brother, he squared his little shoulders and reached into Big Brother's backpack and pulled Umbrella out as if he was Arthur and Umbrella was the legendary Excalibur. As the hoard was about to pounce, Little Brother slashed, whacked and basically pummeled them.

The gang was so shocked at Little Brother's boldness that they froze.

Big Brother looked in disbelief at the umbrella-wielding hero and shouted, "Let's get outta here!"

Jumping on their bikes, they darted away from Snake and his violent gang.

"Oh no, what's Ma gonna say? wailed Big Brother. How am I going to explain how I look? She's gonna kill me!"

Better her than these ghouls, thought Umbrella.

Behind the brothers, footsteps and loud shouts could be heard in the dark.

"Don't look back," said Big Brother. "Keep going!" he panted.

The two brothers peddled furiously in the dark night and longed for their home.

After a few moments, the pounding footsteps and curse-infused shouts of Snake and his crew faded into the black night. Big Brother stole a look over his shoulder. "Whew!" he said. "That could have really been bad!"

He looked over at brave Little Brother and said, "Hey, you saved my butt!"

Little Brother lifted Umbrella high over his head and said, "Super Umbrella to the rescue!"

As Little Brother tried to balance his bike, he clutched the handle bars with both hands and dropped Umbrella into the wet street.

Looking down, Little Brother let out a small yelp. "Oh no, turn around! We have to go back and get it!"

"No way, Little Bro, leave it! Those guys could be hiding anywhere. I wouldn't want you to get hurt," he said in a tender voice.

Umbrella looked up from the wet street and saw Big Brother reach over and playfully toss Little Brother's hair. "We make a good team."

Under the street light, Umbrella watched as their shadows grew smaller. He resentfully gazed at them as the brothers disappeared into the dark. Their figures would reappear and disappear as they passed under the street lights. It was as if someone was playing with a light switch. With each passing second, the brothers grew tinier and tinier and their laughter and voices grew dim until there was nothing. No sound, no light…no anything.

Hey, what about me, thought Umbrella.

He was panicked. Rather than considering the close call with danger the brothers had narrowly escaped, Umbrella just lay there, moaning and whining. Lying in the middle of the street, he tried to roll over closer to the sidewalk.

How am I going to get to The Statue of Liberty? Someone get me back to that dumb Mannequin. At least I was the most popular and famous umbrella when I was in the display window. Why are all of these bad things happening to me? I was made for greatness! Maybe if I try to open up and start rolling, I can fly again! Great idea, me! I am such a genius!

Before he was able to move an inch, a huge SUV ran over Umbrella.

Ouch! was the last thing heard before Umbrella lost consciousness.

☂

Dawn rose, with a misty hazy warmth that made the day feel heavy. Humid still air made Umbrella feel immovable and stuck. Umbrella looked around and surveyed his surroundings and immediately realized he was in danger. He was lying in the dirty street and he was broken and damaged.

How did I get here, he wondered. *Oh, that's right! Little Brother dropped me in the middle of the street! It's that brat's fault that I was run over by a monster truck! Why is everything so hard for me,* sulked Umbrella.

He was bruised and some of his fabric had been torn. In the distance, Umbrella heard something like glass tinkling. A tiny and crackly voice was singing something, much as a child would sound. "Happy Birthday to you, Merry Birthday dear Scarlet, it's a birthday for you…" sang a faraway voice.

The confusing lyrics and the odd humming grew louder. It was coming closer and closer. Slowly, out of the fog, appeared Old Lady. She was covered in dirty, torn clothes and she pushed a shopping cart filled with things that looked unfamiliar from a distance. Before Umbrella could see what they were, she was upon him and snatched him off of the dirty ground. Umbrella was shoved into the rusty shopping cart filled with dozens of cans and bottles. An old, green army blanket filled an enormous part of the shopping cart. But astonishingly, there were other items. Umbrella found himself rendered speechless. He was in a shopping cart filled with dozens of umbrellas!

I am finally with my own kind! I won't need to convince them of my obvious superiority. They will see my greatness, he thought and a smug smile spread across his tatterred fabric.

There were tall umbrellas, tiny ones, a large one made of intricate plaid, a short black one, one with a white kitten with an enormous head on it and a clear plastic one that looked like half a ball. And in one of the corners- a red umbrella with a delicate bamboo handle.

Whoa, thought Umbrella. *She's gorgeous!*

Umbrella stared at the red umbrella for a long time until she noticed and she quickly turned a deeper shade of red. Umbrella had never seen so many umbrellas in one place and they were all so unique. He thought that he would like to hear all of their different stories, but he reconsidered. *Why bother?* Umbrella smirked. *She's the only one that looks interesting.* Umbrella would flash her his most charming smile but she would lower her eyes and look away. Umbrella wanted to move closer to her but he was aching. His spines felt like they had been turned inside out. But miraculously, they had stayed in place.

I wish I looked like I did when Old Man first created me. I was strong, perfect and shiny. She wouldn't have been able to resist me, Umbrella fantasized.

For a brief moment, Umbrella allowed himself to remember the old, firm hands that had so caringly and expertly assembled him. He remembered the barking of Team Leader and how Old Man's hands shook as he tenderly covered his spines in the silk-like fabric. Umbrella felt an unfamiliar feeling come over him.

It was something close to gratitude but before Umbrella let it wash over him he thought, *Ha. Old Man was such a fool. Look at me now. How am I going to be the change in the world stuck in this filthy shopping cart? But it wouldn't be all bad if I could meet that red umbrella. I'll impress her,* he thought with abundant confidence.

The noon sun was high in the sky. *We have been walking for hours,* Umbrella speculated. The blazing sun was beating down on him and Old Lady's singing was like a lullaby. The sun, the singing and the soft pace of the shopping cart were the perfect recipe for a nap. Still very bruised from the night before, Umbrella fell into a feverish slumber.

Hours later, Umbrella woke.

How long have I been asleep? Where are we, he wondered.

Old Lady had stopped in an alley. There was a large, green dumpster and trash everywhere. She was pulling umbrella after umbrella out of the messy cart. He saw that the green army blanket had been laid out on the dirty concrete. Old Lady grabbed him and tossed him to the filthy ground. She had opened up several of the other umbrellas and had arranged them on the ground in a semi-circle next to dumpster.

Umbrella saw the red one and mumbled a quick prayer, *please, please next to her!*

And before he knew it, Old Lady was opening him up. It was extremely painful. However, almost as if she sensed that he was hurt, she placed him gently next to the red umbrella.

Yes, thought Umbrella. He tried to look around but was still in considerable pain from last night's adventure. *Why did Little Brother have to use me as a weapon,* he complained.

The sun was beginning to set and the tall buildings cast a shadow over the busy streets. Old Lady was still arranging more umbrellas until there was just a small opening left. She crawled through it and laid down on the green army blanket. Within a few moments, her breathing had slowed and she had fallen into a deep sleep.

"Where are we? I feel like we have been walking for hours!" Umbrella grumbled.

The short black umbrella next to him answered. "We have been, fella. You've been out the whole time! We're in an alley now, kid! Every night, Old Lady finds a place where she can hide away from people and she makes herself a house out of us. It ain't a bad life because every day we go someplace else. It's an adventure. We are her protection. By the way, I'm Shorty." he said.

Umbrella looked over at the compact and friendly umbrella and moved away from him. The last thing Umbrella wanted to do was to make friends with this insignificant object.

Something must have happened to him in the factory, he mused. *He is only half of an umbrella,* Umbrella thought quite cruelly.

After the audacity of Shorty's attempt at friendship, Umbrella thought that now would be the perfect time to reveal his superiority and his amazing purpose to this group of ordinary umbrellas.

I don't care to meet any of these clearly, inferior umbrellas. Except for that red umbrella, he reflected. *She is so beautiful. When she finds out that I am going to be famous, she won't be able to resist me.*

"Hello," Umbrella announced, clearing his throat. "I am the Umbrella that was created to change the world."

Umbrella made this incredible announcement expecting all of the other umbrellas, especially the red one, to clap and cheer.

"Get a load of this guy. Did you hear him? He's gonna change the world!" Shorty said with a smirk.

With that, all the umbrellas started to rock in a chorus of laughter. Even the red one was giggling.

"Should we call you Mr. Wonderful or something?" teased Shorty as he gave Umbrella a good-natured wink.

More laughter erupted from the crowd. "Hey fella, I am just kidding. We are all friends here! Seriously, what would you really like us to call you?" Shorty asked in a friendly voice.

Umbrella glared at Shorty. "I really don't care what you call me. How dare you misfits laugh at me? I was created to do more than just get pushed around in a dirty cart. Are you blind? Look at me. I am amazing. I'll bet none of you have ever flown. Well, I have! I flew over an entire campus! I was designed for better things than being here with all of you. I am destined to be the most famous umbrella on the entire planet!" proclaimed Umbrella.

After Umbrella's tone-deaf speech, a soft voice spoke. It was the red one.

"Hey." she said. "Don't be so angry. Shorty is just kidding. He is really kind. And the rest are really nice, too. So is Old Lady. She is the nicest lady I have ever had the privilege to know. We are all she has to help her make a place to rest each night. We keep her safe. By the way, I'm Scarlet," she whispered.

I can die now, thought Umbrella. *She spoke to me! I must be in umbrella heaven,* he thought as his anger quickly disappeared.

"Hi there, Scarlet." Umbrella said in his most charming voice. "Why don't you just call me Umbrella? You know, instead of The-Umbrella-that-changed-the world."

Scarlet suppressed a giggle. She realized that Umbrella was serious. She had never met an umbrella that was so conceited. She turned away from Umbrella and became very quiet and pretended to be asleep. He could see that she was rebuffing him.

What is the matter with her, he thought. *Why would anyone want to live in a shopping cart?*

Umbrella's confusion quickly turned to frustration. *Fine,* he fumed. *It's her loss.*

The sounds of the bustling city were muffled as night fell. The alley was silent except for the occasional door springing open and the sound of someone opening up the dumpster and throwing garbage into it. Old Lady was asleep on the dirty green blanket and occasionally would stir and mumble something from her broken dreams.

Once Scarlett knew that she was sleeping deeply, she decided to tell Umbrella the story of Old Lady.

Maybe if he knows the truth, he will understand how we all are giving her shelter, thought Scarlet naively. *Maybe he will see that she needs us to protect her.*

She turned back toward Umbrella and spoke to him. "She is a very sweet lady. I belong to her." she explained.

"Well, I guess we all do, don't we?" smirked Umbrella.

"No, before," she firmly stated. "It was a long time ago. I belonged to her before she left her warm home and her wonderful life behind."

Then Scarlet spoke patiently to Umbrella. She told him the story as if he was a young child. He stared at this sweet umbrella but really wasn't listening to her. All of the other umbrellas remained respectfully quiet. They had always wanted to hear the story of Old Lady and Scarlet.

"You see, I was her original. We once lived in a beautiful home where she would keep me in a blue vase by an enormous heavy door. She had a Mister who kept a carved wooden cane in the vase with me. When they would go walking, Mister would carry the cane and she would carry me. Even if it didn't look like rain! She loved to have me with her. Then one day, Mister didn't come home. I forgot when it happened because it was so very long ago. She stayed in her room and cried from early in the morning until late at night. We never went outside anymore. But one day, Old Lady put on her coat and picked me up from the vase. I was so happy that maybe life would be kind to her again. I thought that perhaps she was getting better. She opened the big wooden door and we just started to walk. That was that. At first, I was relieved that Old Lady didn't cry anymore. She would sing her little song and I was so happy. She had stopped crying but sadly, she never spoke again. It was as if all of her sorrow took her voice away. We never went back to our home and we have been living like this for a very long time. I don't mind so much. You see, we are all she has to protect her." Scarlett said simply.

Scarlet nodded respectfully to all of the umbrellas around her. "I don't know what will happen but I know this...every time she makes me into her house for the night I feel worthwhile. I know that I am helping her," said Scarlet.

Umbrella was suddenly irritated by Scarlet.

"So that's it? I mean, if this is good enough for you, I guess that's your choice. But someone as fine and well-designed as you deserves a much better life. Honestly, Scarlett, I would be really angry at her if she forced me to live in the streets. And ashamed! You live a filthy nomads' life!" said Umbrella in a raised voice. He was angry at this beautiful red umbrella for her selflessness and compassion.

"I mean, Scarlet, don't you see how beautifully you have been made? You can't convince me that being stuffed in this filthy shopping cart with all of these other wretched umbrellas is what you want from life. So being this old lady's house every night is enough for you? You can't be real. What are you, some sort of saint or angel? Well, I am not. I hate being her house, as you call it! I was designed for greater things!" Umbrella announced.

Scarlet and all of the umbrellas were stunned. Even the hardest of hearts would be softened by Old Lady's sad life. Scarlet began to quietly weep. Everyone was silent. For once, Umbrella was quiet too. He was simmering at all of their ignorance. He was bitter that Scarlet couldn't see his celebrity and the places that he could take her.

Finally, one brave umbrella broke the silence. Plaid Gentleman addressed Scarlet in an aristocratic British accent. "Dearest Scarlet, thank you for sharing that compelling narrative. I know I speak for all, that it was a complete privilege to learn of Old Lady's previous genteel life. It is a tragedy that she lives as she does. However, I am honored to be of service. I do recall being quite put out when my owner tossed me away. He was a shallow chap and merely carried me because I conveyed status. Imagine my joy and gratitude when you and Old Lady walked by the rubbish bin and saved my life. As for the arrogant and heartless Umbrella, I hope that he finds himself in other company. Immediately. He does not deserve to be in the presence of any lady."

Scarlet wiped away her tears and gave the noble Plaid Gentleman a small smile of appreciation.

Umbrella's anger was explosive. *How dare "Plaid Guy" tell those lies! I have a heart,* Umbrella justified to himself. Umbrella began to panic when he realized that Scarlet might never leave with him.

I must make a grand proclamation! This is my last chance to convince her that I am the greatest umbrella in the world, he told himself as his thoughts scrambled. Immediately, he began to blather to Scarlet that *they* were different and superior than the other umbrellas in the cart. He recklessly and fruitlessly continued to point out all of the other umbrellas imperfections. No umbrella was spared by his scathing and cruel critiques.

Umbrella's final and crushing blow came with his announcement to the family of umbrellas. "I wasn't about to waste this incredible news on the likes of you but I suppose one day you will know! Instead of living in a filthy shopping cart pushed around by a homeless woman, I will be magnificently hovering above The Statue of Liberty! So everyone in the world will know I was created to be the Umbrella that changed the world!"

With that, the entire umbrella audience convulsed in a cacophony of guffaws so loud that stray dogs were heard howling. Every umbrella was rocking with the kind of laughter that approached hysteria. Everyone but Scarlet. She was looking at him, slowly shaking her head as a lone tear ran down her beautiful bamboo handle and landed on the alley floor.

Spent and misunderstood, Umbrella stopped speaking. He gazed at the makeshift house he had become a part of and looked at his fellow umbrellas and spoke one last time.

"You'll see. I will be the change in this world. And not a change that makes some crazy lady happy...I will do it to make me happy. And when I am famous, all of you will regret how you laughed at me. Some more than others." Umbrella finished pointedly, glaring at Scarlet.

Self-satisfied and unrepentant, Umbrella shut his eyes and longed for the gift of sleep. Tomorrow he would find a way to get away from these losers. He had wasted too much of his valuable time on them. Especially Scarlet.

The day heralded with the sound of Old Lady opening up the dumpster. The morbid creaking, rummaging and subsequent crash of its lid announced that she had found her breakfast. Once she finished, she gathered the umbrellas in nimble and rapid succession. She arranged them quickly into the shopping cart. When she came to Scarlet, though, Old Lady picked her up tenderly and smoothed down her red fabric and placed her back into the far corner. As Old Lady roamed her uncharted path, Scarlet served as her beacon as she searched for her next resting spot. Umbrella was the last one to be collected. Old Lady picked up Umbrella and closed him. Her hands were very gentle. She smoothed down his torn and battered fabric and placed him under the cart with the green army blanket.

Good, Umbrella sulked. *I am glad I am not with them.*

Umbrella heard Shorty say, "She put him down there with the blanket! Maybe Old Lady knew what that jerk said to all of us last night."

"Very well then, for the lone chap." said Plaid Gentleman, with his crisp British accent. "If you recall, he clearly believed that we were not in his league, after all."

Moments later, Umbrella heard a soft sigh.

Scarlet gently murmured, "I still feel sorry for him."

Umbrella said nothing. They walked for miles.Through the hot city and past pretty houses with gardens filled with bright blooms which gave Umbrella's nose temporary relief from the blanket's stench. Finally, after hours of walking, their pilgrimage came to an end. The shopping cart had stopped but Old Lady didn't start the construction of her umbrella house. They were on the edge of a seemingly endless park. It was green and lush with beautiful flowers that leaned against stones carved onto beautiful statues and tablets.

Ha, thought Umbrella. *This has to be the entrance to where they keep The Statue of Liberty! I told everyone that this was why I was created! Greatness and fame are right around the corner! Wait until they see me atop Lady Liberty! They all will be sorry!*

Old Lady walked a short way to a stone bench that stood in the middle of the verdant green lawn. She sat down and reached into her shabby pocket and pulled out a crushed arrangement of flowers that she must have found in the dumpster. They must have been thrown away from one of the restaurants that backed up into the alley. Somberly, Old Lady laid them on the stone bench. With a deep and sorrowful sigh, she stood and slowly walked back to the rusty cart.

Suddenly, Umbrella felt the old woman's bony fingers around him. Old Lady lifted him from the bottom of the cart and carried him over to the bench where she had placed the wilted flowers. She placed Umbrella under the stone bench. Without a word, she left him there.

Umbrella heard the shopping cart with it's tingling cans and bottles and Old Lady's sing-song voice becoming dimmer and dimmer. *She kept all of those other umbrellas with her but me,* Umbrella considered feeling insulted.

Fine, he thought bitterly. *No one even said goodbye to me. No one cares about me. Not even Scarlet. I'll show them! I need to find that statue!*

First, Umbrella tried to roll further into the park. *Well, this might take some time but at least I am closer to becoming famous!*

Glancing at the sea of white cemetery markers he thought, *These monuments are small and puny. I thought The Statue of Liberty soared miles into the sky! She must be further inside the park.*

But try as he might, he was stuck. He tried prying his spines open. Again, he met failure. He tried to roll from under the stone bench. He barely moved an inch.

Umbrella wasn't beat yet. His performance in front of the clueless and forgettable other umbrellas had inspired him. He still felt sorry about losing Scarlet but he justified her indifference.

Scarlet was naive and silly. I could never be happy with someone who belonged to a homeless person, he justified. *Although she was beautiful, I am the only umbrella that was designed to be the greatest in the world. And I wasn't about to share my spot above The Statue of Liberty! Maybe*

I will become the eight Wonder of the World! Well, I guess it was all for a reason.

His confidence was at its pinnacle. He was going to be atop the most iconic figure in America.

After a long day of tries, Umbrella decided to call it a night. He snuggled against the stone bench. *I will be part of history tomorrow,* Umbrella told himself. He fell quickly into a self-satisfied slumber.

A violent thunderstorm shook him awake. The rain came in sheets that seemed to fall sideways. Lighting flashes illuminated the statues in grotesque ways that had Umbrella retreating closer to the stone bench. Several times during the stormy night, Umbrella would be yanked away by ferocious gusts of lighting charged winds that threatened to break his remaining intact spines but somehow he would muster the strength to stay on the ground and cling to the stone bench. It was a terrifying and sleepless night that seemed it would never end. Umbrella was afraid. Truly afraid.

I think this really might be the end of me, he darkly thought. *And I am so close to fulfilling my dreams of fame.*

A wave of self-pity washed over him. He cowardly shook with panic. After many hours hiding from the horrific storm, he fell into a nightmarish sleep.

Daybreak finally arrived. The world was washed clean. The verdant grass sparkled as if diamonds had been scattered among its blades. The magnificent trees looked full and lush as if they had been filled with cool water. A blue and cloudless sky featured a blazing sun. The ghoulish statues from last night had been transformed into pristine sculptures. Umbrella could see angels, tall obelisks and statues adorned with garlands. In the distance, was a sea of countless white tombstones standing in timeless and perfect formation.

Oh no, Umbrella thought. *I am not anywhere near The Statue of Liberty! Could this be Arlington Cemetery? Why did Old Lady leave me here?*

He closed his eyes against the brilliance that surrounded him. The light held a brutal clarity. It hurt Umbrella to see such purity. He scrunched closer to the bench.

What is happening to me? he wondered. *Why am I feeling so insignificant?*

I've got to get out of here!

As his confidence waned, Umbrella clung to his spot under the stone bench. He was shaking and sweating.

Umbrella snickered, *This is ironic. I am having my first panic attack in the very place that our bravest men and women are laid to rest.*

For the first time, Umbrella felt something new and unknown to him. Umbrella began to understand the harsh truth. His life had been entirely devoted to the superficial pursuit for celebrity. Umbrella knew that every opportunity that had been given to him to do something kind or unselfish for the people he had encountered, he had ignored.

I never raised a spine to help anyone, Umbrella ruefully admitted. He bowed his head in shame.

Umbrella realized that he would never get another chance to do anything worthy of what his creator saw in him. He had failed Old Man.

"Why did he tell me that I was the Umbrella that would change the world?" he whispered.

These first honest words rustled like a warm wind among the solemn landscape.

Real tears of repentance flowed from him. Umbrella was ashamed of himself and his selfishness and conceit.

Remembering Old Man, Mannequin, Dante, Daisy, Mary, BusDriver Frank, Broom Man and his friends, Big and Little Brother, Old Lady, Shorty, Plaid Gentleman and with a deep and regretful sigh, Umbrella whispered the word, "Scarlet."

His heart was broken for everyone who had ever held him, met him or had even seen him. *I was so blind. I have hurt so many and won't be able to make it right. My time here is almost done.* Tears welled up in his eyes as he thought of all of his selfish actions.

Umbrella's damage and injuries from last night's storm were massive. He deduced that his splintered spines and the rips and tears in his once magnificent fabric were permanent. Umbrella understood his fate. He would never get the chance to be the change in the world or in anyone's life. Umbrella's sorrow was deep and complete. He held in his heart the worst feeling of all- regret.

The morning's cool beginning was replaced with an unrelenting sun that burned into his inner spine. Umbrella tried to push himself from under the stone bench. Weak and beaten, he looked out onto the vibrant green field and felt immense gratitude that Old Lady had left him in this peaceful place.

Old Lady did much more for me than I ever deserved, he thought. *Truly, she was an angel and all of her umbrellas were noble, caring, and kind. I thought Snake was a monster. No, the monster is me.*

Umbrella closed his eyes. He was too ashamed to look out at the monuments of those who had sacrificed their lives for others. He knew he would never get the chance to do anything noble or selfless. *I don't deserve to be here among all of these heroes.*

Sometime later he heard a small whimper. Opening his eyes he saw that a tiny girl was sitting on the stone bench above him. She hid her face in her little hands and was sobbing.

I wonder if she is lost. Where is her family?

Before Umbrella's next thought, a deep rumbling voice was heard. An older man walked toward the bereft little girl. He used loving words as he approached and sat down next to her and pulled her close.

"Dear, dear Phoebe, it's ok to cry." he consoled.

"I promised Mama I wouldn't. I told her I would be brave just like Daddy." she cried.

"No Darling, Mama doesn't expect that. Nonnie and I have not stopped crying either. Your Daddy wouldn't want this for you." Grandfather said.

The little girl cried, "But I don't want to hear them, Grandfather."

"Hear what Sweetie?" Grandfather asked softly.

"You know, the guns. I don't want to hear that scary sound!" she cried.

"Phoebe, Phoebe, of course, you don't. I understand but that is the way that we honor all of our heroes. It's not fair that a little girl has to say goodbye to her Daddy. He was the bravest man I have ever known. He fought so that all of us could live in a free and beautiful country. He loved you so very much. He will always be with you, do you understand?" he said as he reached to hold his granddaughter.

"No, Grandfather! How will I know when he is near? How will I ever know if he sees me or hears me?" she cried as if her little heart would break.

Umbrella had a profound feeling of helplessness. He tried to open his spines. The pain was crushing. *Maybe I could help her,* he thought. *Perhaps if they see me, I could do something to make things better!*

Umbrella tried to push himself away from the stone bench. But he was so broken and torn that he could barely move. The physical pain was excruciating. Yet, the pain in his soul seemed bottomless. Umbrella knew that his life was waning. Anguish engulfed him. *Why was I so selfish? I wasted my life chasing a fantasy of fame! And now I can't even help this little girl!*

Phoebe stopped her tears for one second and looked across the green field. People dressed in black stood around a casket covered in a bold American flag. A lone woman sat stoically in a chair. Her veiled head was bowed. The Honor Guard stood nearby. Their rifles gleamed in the sweltering sunshine and were at the ready for the ceremonial salute.

A shudder came from the little girl and the Grandfather lifted her onto his lap.

"They are about to do it, Grandfather." she said burying her tiny face into his dark jacket.

"I know, Honey. Here, I'll put my hands over your ears." said GrandFather.

Just then, GrandFather looked down. He noticed Umbrella peeking out from under the stone bench.

"Look Phoebe, an Umbrella! Let's open it up and it will protect you!" he said, almost laughing.

"An umbrella, GrandFather, when it's sunny out!" said Phoebe, looking around as if embarrassed.

"It's the perfect idea. I will hold it over us and you can cover your ears and everything will be ok!" he said.

GrandFather picked up Umbrella. His old and warm hands reminded Umbrella of his creator. Before Umbrella could recall the words whispered to him so long ago GrandFather began to open Umbrella. Umbrella felt white-hot pain as his broken spines tried to accommodate but he was too broken to open completely. An entire side of him was caved in and his once magnificent fabric was dirty, torn, and tattered. Even in his battered condition, Umbrella was able to cast a shadow that shielded the tiny girl and the GrandFather from the glaring hot sun. Most importantly, Umbrella protectively blocked the sorrowful scene below.

Umbrella felt like screaming. His spines were broken and he was afraid he might collapse. GrandFather's strong hands made Umbrella feel a little more steady and confident. Umbrella looked down upon Phoebe.

Poor little one, he thought.

And somewhere deep within Umbrella came a foreign feeling. This feeling was growing, bubbling up from a place Umbrella never knew existed within his frame. The searing pain in his spine seemed to dull as he looked down at Grandfather and especially Phoebe. She had her tiny hands cupped tightly against her ears and her head was down as curls covered her face.

I MUST DO SOMETHING TO HELP. I MUST DO THIS ONE LAST THING! Umbrella desperately thought as he tried to ignore the pain.

Grandfather held Umbrella in one hand and with the other, stroked Phoebe's head tenderly. With all of the strength left in Umbrella's broken being, he stretched out his mangled spine and opened himself up completely, choosing to sacrifice himself to protect the tiny girl.

Umbrella felt more of his fabric tearing. The pain was intense. But Umbrella's only thought was for the little girl and her sorrow. Phoebe had buried her face into Grandfather's jacket. GrandFather reached into his pocket and pulled out a handkerchief for the little girl.

"Here Sweetie," he said kindly.

Phoebe looked at the pocket GrandFather pulled the handkerchief from and her crying ceased.

She let out a gasp, "It's Daddy. He is here! Look, Umbrella is showing me that my Daddy will always be with me!"

Looking down at his dark jacket, Grandfather saw it, too.

"Good Lord," he whispered.

A golden beam from the bright sun overhead was shining through Umbrella's torn fabric. The rays from the sweltering sun had traced a perfect heart upon Grandfather's dark jacket.

"This is a miracle," Grandfather said reverently.

The gun salute had begun. Under Umbrella, Phoebe and Grandfather were protected and peaceful. Respectfully, they sat as the sound of rifle fire echoed around them. And yet, the little girl remained calm. She watched, in awe, as Grandfather slowly turned Umbrella. As he shifted Umbrella's position, the heart would appear in a new place. The same heart that Umbrella had made on Grandfather's jacket, now shone on Phoebe's small hands and then on her cheek. The little girl was serene and on her face was a smile.

The playing of Taps had finished and many of the mourners had moved away from the gravesite and into their cars. The lone woman sat alone by the casket and was grasping the folded American flag. Grandfather lifted Phoebe to her feet, and gently placed what remained of Umbrella, under his arm.

They walked down the green slope toward the gravesite, and before they reached the solemn woman, Grandfather knelt and looked at the little girl and said," Here you go, my brave Phoebe."

GrandFather handed Umbrella to the little girl and said, "Now let's go and show your Mama that your Daddy is safe in heaven."

Oh no, Umbrella thought, barely able to breathe. *I can't bear it. I am too broken to be opened. I can't do it again.*

Umbrella felt his strength fading and he knew he was near his end. Yet, Umbrella was desperate to help this wounded family.

I have wasted so much of my life. I am so sorry, Umbrella lamented as he went limp. His breathing slowed and became shallow.

Phoebe clutched Umbrella close to her chest and walked purposefully and hopefully toward her grieving mother. Umbrella could feel Phoebe's tiny heart beating rapidly. The electrical pulses from the little girl seemed to transfer a healing energy unto Umbrella's twisted spines and torn fabric. He could feel himself growing stronger.

How can this be happening? Could the beats of her little heart be healing me? Umbrella wondered.

As Phoebe strode purposefully toward her heartbroken mother, Umbrella recognized himself in the worn woman. At last, Umbrella truly understood why he had been created. Remembering Mannequin, Dante, Daisy, BusDriver Frank, Mary, Broom Man and his friends, Big and Little Brother, Old Lady, the beautiful Scarlet, the umbrellas in the cart, Grandfather, and especially Phoebe gave Umbrella newfound clarity and strength. He understood that everyone he had met had been placed in his life for a divine reason. They were all part of this purposeful plan that was unfolding before him. Umbrella was overcome with humility and gratefulness for this final task.

As Phoebe climbed gingerly onto her Mother's lap and Grandfather looked on, the sun shone high in the blistering afternoon sky. When her bewildered mother noticed what Phoebe was holding she glanced, quizzically over her shoulder at Grandfather. He held up his finger and mouthed the words, "Just wait." Phoebe lifted Umbrella toward the sun and moved her little fingers up Umbrella's broken spine until he miraculously opened. The Mother gasped. The same perfect heart appeared on her long black dress.

As Umbrella looked down at their faces, one smiling and one shocked, he whispered, "Thank you for creating me to be the change I wished to see in the World."

The End☂

on can be obtained
₹.com
₹1
/730